TRANSPOETHICALBODY
A Book of Black Trans* Erotic Poetry

TRANS CORPO ÉTICO
[poesia erótica trans preta]

TIELY
Translated By
Bruna Barros and Jess Oliveira
With Illustrations By Ani Ganzala

ISBN: 979-8-9872776-0-7 (Paperback)
ISBN: 979-8-9872776-2-1 (eBook)

First English Translation Printed Edition 2023
Améfrica Press
P.O. Box 24647
Baltimore, MD 21214 USA
www.amefricapress.com

First Published in Portuguese in São Paulo, Brazil in 2020 as:
Trans Corpo Ético: poesia erótica trans preta by Tiely Santos
Publisher: Ciclo Contínuo Editorial: www.ciclocontinuoeditorial.com
ISBN 978-65-992307-6-9

DEDICATION

i thank and dedicate this book to my mother, Dona Fátima, who always encouraged me to read, from comic books to the Bible!
to my sisters and brothers who enjoyed the best of the 1970s and 1980s! to my older brothers who couldn't hide their erotic magazines from me! (lol) to my literature and Portuguese teachers!
to all and everyone who have always been and believed in my path!

TRANSLATION NOTE

Jess Oliveira

Bruna Barros

> *A belated mouth talks over my body (ex)claims Speaking*
> *softly, spilling some hot, volcanic verses Fire in words, a*
> *husky voice that shakes, i am flame.*
> Tiely, RHYMING ON YOU

> *i devour your commas, your periods, and your question marks*
> *walking out unnoticed, i don't leave a trace behind*
> *silent, weak in the corner, hallucinating every line in mind*
> *i want your avid kisses in exclamation marks*
> Tiely, WANDERING WRITING

> *[...] translation is the most intimate act of reading.*
> Spivak[1]

After we got the request from the editor Tanya Saunders to write about the translation, we thought that it would be important to

[1] See Spivak, Gayatri Chakravorty. The Politics of Translation, 1992.

the English-speaking readers to become more intimate with the translation process from Brazilian Portuguese into English. We decided therefore to highlight some aspects and some decision-making processes aroused by the poems and the vocabulary deployed by Tiely.

We have been discussing in our Research Group Traduzindo no Atlântico Negro, at Federal University of Bahia, that a procedure to translate texts (both written and oral) by Black authors is to be aware of the paths the very text shows us. What are the messages being conveyed by the texts? What lies in the history and between the lines? How do they convey the messages? How does the author deal with and dwell in the language?

Pleasure and bliss are present in Tiely's poetry, so pleasure and bliss must also be on the translators' fingers. We found ourselves looking at all the words the poet uses for pleasure in Brazilian Portuguese, tasting their sounds to come up with different alternatives, as many of them do not share their sensual connotation in English. It was a lot like finding new words to call lovers.

In this sense, one of the first aspects that instigated us about translating this book was thinking about how to deal with terms of endearment which are very tied to intimate contexts in the source language, such as *pretinha* [preˈtʃiɲɐ; preˈtiɲɐ], a loving (and contested) way of calling Black womxn/lovers. Then we also had the ever-present *sapatão* [sapaˈtẽw̃], a term used by people in the lesbian identity spectrum, which appears here as *sapata* [saˈpatɐ], one of its variations.[2] We decided not to translate either of these terms, in order to convey the specificity of the people, the places, and the relationships inside and surrounding the book's poetical body. This brings us to the title:

Trans Corpo Ético *[poesia erótica trans preta]* consists of a word play – an agglomeration or assemblage of words – containing and meaning "trans", "cor" [color], "corpo" [body], "ético" [ethical], "poético" [poetical]. In the translation, we ended up losing "cor", however the loss was soon recovered in the subtitle. *TRANSPOETHICALBODY: A Book of Black Trans* Erotic Poetry* was a title we came up with in conversation with both the author and the editor. We believe the title may help the reader make the connection(s) that exist in the Brazilian Portuguese title.

Among other words, the verb *alucinar*, literally "hallucinate", had such a strong presence in the book. It was deployed with many meanings, whether as a description of the feeling of being together or as great sexual bliss. Instead of using its literal translation, we walked attentively through the dark, much like *aranhas* – [spiders] in Brazilian Portuguese, also a slang for vulva, which turns this organ so often placed as passive into a many-legged mysterious predator, as in Tiely's *Corporeal*'s "sea of spiders" –, carefully finding our ways to describe the intimate sensations we find with each other under dim lights or under the warm sun.

For us, it is always a bliss to translate poetry. We hope the

[2]See Barros, Bruna and Jess Oliveira. 2020. "Black Sapatão Translation Practices: Healing Ourselves a Word Choice at a Time". Caribbean Review of Gender Studies, Issue 14: 43–52.

English-speaking public find the bliss on the words and feel the
encounter of tongues in this bilingual edition.

EDITOR'S NOTE

Améfrica Press is honored to introduce Transpoethicalbody: A book of Black Trans* Erotic Poetry, by Tiely. It is our inaugural publication! In this launch of the first book, and the Press, i would like to give a special thanks to Stephanie Andrea Allen, founder of BLF Press, for her mentorship and support. Through her, i learned how to build this press, and how to publish my first book. Without this tremendous act of solidarity, this book would not be in your hand today. We certainly look forward to collaborating with BLF Press in the future, but in the meantime, stay tuned to our websites (www.amefricapress.com and www. blfpress.com). The spirit of collaboration for the uplifting of Black folks across the diaspora, in our diversity, is also the goal of Améfrica Press.

The aim, the desire, of Améfrica Press is to bring to an English-speaking audience the work of Portuguese and Spanish- speaking Black artists, writers and scholars from Latin America and the Caribbean. We give thanks for the possibility of interrupting the linguistic, epistemic and geopolitical borders that continue to influence, and limit, our lives across the Améfricas. This happens in terms of how we understand/ experience our spiritual and embodied selves, our individual and collective agency. The name of Améfrica Press is based on "Améfrica Ladina," an important concept coined by the Brazilian Black feminist scholar and activist Lélia Gonzalez. She coined the term to decenter the Eurocentric story about origins of the Americas, in order to center the African and Indigenous roots of our contemporary Améfrican nations. The publication of Transpoethicalbody is one of these moments of connection. As the Festival Afro Latinidades has posited - it is an opportunity to work towards the reintegration of the Afro-descendant posse in the Améfricas; remembering that our collective paths come from afar.

In Transpoethicalbody, Tiely refocuses our attention on bodies enjoying pleasure, on feeling, offering and receiving pleasure. African and Afro-diasporic folks rarely have a moment to disconnect from the anti-Black world that we inhabit, to focus on ourselves, our dreams, our desires. An additional gift of this book is how Black bodies show up in the text. There is no clear relation between body and gender identity. Instead, there is the affirmation of Black bodies, especially Black trans* bodies, in all of our diversity. This allows for all of us to capture glimpses of diverse selves in this work. The images in this book present another layer of meaning and sensation to the texts. The texts and images display the range of emotions connected to feeling self love, and how that love is, or sometimes isn't, reflected back. This text creates another rupture within an anti-Black world, space to just feel the feels. The original text included photographs of trans* bodies expressing emotions such as grace, rage and vulnerability. The images are full of life and feelings which challenge the oftentime simplistic representations of trans* and Black folks. This compilation is a love letter, a gift to Black folks, especially people living in trans* bodies in this world.

Transpoethicalbody is not only a poetry collection it is also care, it is existence, it is feeling, it is a celebration of Black and Black trans* bodies. It is a challenge to the thingification of our bodies, it is a manifesto! Tiely's book is not only a provocation to the cis public, but also a provocation to people who inhabit this world in trans* and gender non-conforming bodies. It is a reminder to honor our bodies, by seeing them as sacred and worthy of pleasure. Thus, we cannot forget about the most important provocation of this work: joy. Enjoy this book, read the poems, the images, touch yourself, touch somebody else while reading this book, or just imagine. Whatever you do, remember that this book is an invitation to pleasure! Enjoy it! Congratulations, Tiely, for this hot and steamy book. i enjoyed and connected with each word and image. In fact, in order to honor the artwork in the original Portuguese language version of the book, Améfrica Press commissioned artwork from the Bahianx artist Ani Ganzala. This collaboration resulted in all the beautiful images in this book, including the striking cover. The effect is the creation of a stunning compilation of poetry, of erotic poetry, and visual art. Enjoy!

Tanya L. Saunders
Founder, Editor-in-Chief
Améfrica Press

PREFACE

what we do, what we like and what we are.
Sex, sexuality and gender in Tiely's poethical work
by Erica Malunguinho[1]

It is we, mind-body conscious people, the ones who actually know the distinction between sex, sexuality and gender. We know it pretty well from existence itself, we know what we practice, who we feel with and who we are. This is the synthesis of sex, sexuality and gender.

In this wide world there is an intentional confusion concerning these layers of humanity (sex, sexuality, gender) which makes our "outside the box", non-normative, transqueer bodies bear a terrible burden, associating us to promiscuity or, conversely, to compulsory chastity, shame or fear, through the imposition of a sort of taboo when we talk about sex or about eroticism. So, when we do, it is almost as if we confirmed the idea of promiscuity that society has about us.

What Tiely does in this book is exactly raising a call for freedom around something that is so infected with others' bad intentions.

[1] Educator and cultural agitator. She holds a Master's degree in Aesthetics and Art History. She became the first trans state deputy (PSOL political party) elected in Brazil in 2018, with more than 55,000 votes in the state of São Paulo. @ericamalunguinho

He is saying that our non-normative bodies have the right to libido, to eroticism, to romance and everything else we desire concerning sexual and affective experiences. i endorse here my respect to the "A" in our acronym, asexual people, and the diverse ways through which they build their relationships with their (own) being.

To poetize in this book, with so many other brilliant beings, for the full emancipation that is also built through eroticism, speaking desire, being skin and sense, instinct… This is a cry, a loud and clear orgasm. Necessary roars breaking the barriers made by a society that is afraid of itself. Afraid of the experience of living people, who narrate every detail, including the sweet-spicy-hot-warm-lubed of reality.

Transpoethicalbody is for our urgent delight, tasting, breathing, to feel the air of T corporalities as a sacred, whole, full place, for we are bearers of the sweet and the sour of knowing how to live and being who one is.

What we are. Sex too.

(...) Appearances deceive those who freeze and those who burn
For fire and ice are united in the autumn of passions
Hearts chop wood and then prepare themselves for another winter
But the summer that brought them together still lives and transpires there
In the bodies that lie together by the fireplace, in the reticent spring
In the insistent scent of something called love.

CONTENTS

TRANSPOETHICALBODY
A Book of Black Trans* Erotic Poetry

TRANS CORPO ÉTICO
[poesia erótica trans preta]

SOFT BITE

leisurely you undress me and make me yours

whispering deliciously in my ear

you make me feel your soul calling

the sweet taste of flowing honey

your body's the mouth that love calls

it carries the secret kept in your chest

a hidden desire only you feel

your sweaty hands give me fire

your igneous black skin

your sex proclaiming climax

soft bite, my sex throbs

you take my soul in your warm mouth

piercing eyes and a dirty tongue

smoothly sliding, i shiver

pleasure without shame, come quickly and do me!

MORDIDA MACIA

sem esperar você me põe nua e sua
sussurra gostoso em meu ouvido
faz eu sentir sua alma que chama
gosto doce do mel que desliza
seu corpo é foz que o amor conclama
traz o segredo que guarda no peito
desejo escondido que só você sente
suas mãos suadas me transmitem fogo
sua pele negra toda incandescente
seu sexo que proclama o intenso gozo
mordida macia, meu sexo lateja
em sua boca quente, suga minh'alma
olhar penetrante e uma língua safada
que desliza gostosa, arrepio me mata
prazer sem pudor, vem logo e me faça!

i LOVE

your breasts,
chalices of liqueur.
your eyes,
nourishment of my desire.
your arms,
snakes around me,
choking me and
smothering my lust
your legs,
entangling my waist
and holding me in all tenderness.
your sex,
where i dive deep
never losing my breath
giving you no peace of mind
oh… sweet taste of peach
no matter how much time goes by
I'll be always inside you
drinking from your chalices.

AMO

seus seios,
cálices de licor.
seus olhos,
alimento do meu desejo.
seus braços,
serpentes que me rodeiam,
me enforcam
e sufocam meu tesão.
suas pernas que
enlaçam minha cintura
e me segura com toda ternura.
seu sexo,
onde mergulho fundo
sem perder o fôlego,
sem te dar sossego.
ah... sabor doce do pêssego
não importa quanto tempo passe,
sempre estarei em ti
bebendo em seus cálices

RHYMING ON YOU

Reading the verses on your body in detail
Like an intimate, intense, insane line of Braille
With my fingers i slowly feel each part
Sweetly deciphering your desire and soul's sweet art

i trace your soft and wandering lines,
i slide through your path to find what your rose enshrines.
i breathe your fragrant scent that entangles me at times
i come alive in your body that climaxes in my mouth

In a shaky moment we are bliss
Bodies that burn in sensual flames
In the soft wee hours, entwined we kiss

A belated mouth speaks, my whole body exclaims
Speaking softly, spilling some hot, volcanic verses
Fire in words, a husky voice that shakes, i am flame.

VERSANDO EM VOCÊ

Lendo os versos que encontro em seu corpo
Como um Braille intimista, intenso e louco
Com meus dedos tateio cada ponto existente
Decifro seu desejo, sua alma, docemente.

Perfilo por entre suas linhas brandas e sinuosas,
Desfilo pelo seu caminho até chegar em sua rosa.
Respiro seu aroma perfumado que me enrosca
Revivo em seu corpo que em minha boca goza

Num momento trêmulo com você somos prazer.
Corpos que queimam numa sensual combustão
Entrelaçadas e felizes com um suave amanhecer

Uma boca tardia diz frases, todo meu corpo clama.
Falando mansinho alguns versos quentes, vulcânicos
Fogo em palavras, voz rouca que abala, sou chama.

ERRATIC WRITING

i devour your commas, your periods, and your question marks
walking out unnoticed, i don't leave a trace behind
silent, weak in the corner, hallucinating every line in mind
i want your avid kisses in exclamation marks

i desire your lost syntax in my triangle
a circle of delights, i burst into tears, i long
i spell your name, each letter a sweet song
i break down in tongues, languages, each wrangle

it looks like a mad fight, no traces and marks
punctuation on bodies, a rare tattoo
a never ending bite on the mouth too.

i write in thoughtless disregard of soft skin
my fingers, erratic writings, and   only the pen
i offer this bare poem to your body

ESCRITA VADIA

devoro suas vírgulas, seus pontos e interrogações
sem deixar rastro com imperceptíveis passos
surdina na esquina me acabo, alucino os traços
quero seus beijos sôfregos em exclamações

desejo sua sintaxe perdida em meu triângulo,
um círculo de delícias, desando em prantos
soletro seu nome, cada letra um doce canto
acabo-me em línguas, idiomas e solavancos.

parece uma briga louca, sem vestígios e marcas
uma pontuação no corpo, uma tatuagem rara
uma mordida na boca, ação que nunca para.

escrevo sem pensar na extensão da pele macia
a caneta, apenas meus dedos e uma escrita vadia
dedico em seu corpo essa simples poesia.

US

overwhelming is the imagination,
voracious is the freedom
when one has no limits.
our only thought is: total ecstasy.
and the most alluring thing
is when this thought
becomes the purest
carnal reality.
reason no longer exists.
my body is all sensation,
pleasure and sweat
receiving your body
burning in mine.
a seduction game,
joy, transformation.
intense craving.
fierce lovers... us.

NÓS

avassaladora é a imaginação,
voraz é a liberdade
quando não se tem limites.
o pensamento é um só: êxtase total.
e o mais interessante
é quando o pensamento
vira a mais pura da
realidade carnal.
a razão já não existe.
meu corpo é só emoção,
prazer e suor
ao receber seu corpo
ardendo no meu.
jogo de sedução,
gozo, transformação.
vício brutal.
amantes ardentes... nós.

COME!

but come upfront
open-chested, eye to eye
your shy mouth on my thirsty mouth
come!
but come with no guilt, no fear, no clothes...s...
naked soul, in action… and in a love full of carnal delight
come!!
scream… rave on… say you're mine, spank and caress me
relax your body… your mind… this apparently absent soft breeze
emerges when pleasure is unique, when our eyes meet
and heat moistens... the hot parts, which catch fire
a latent flame that throbs, the tongue that sucks turns numb
your black rose is so playful in my adult game
come!!!
don't hold back, my Black queen... leave everything behind and
come!!!!

VEM!

mas vem de frente

de peito aberto, olhos nos olhos

boca tímida na minha boca sedenta

vem!

mas vem sem culpa, sem medo, sem roupa...

nua em alma, em atos... e num amor que na carne sente o gozo

vem!!

grita... alucina... diga que és minha, bate e acaricia

relaxa o corpo... a mente... a brisa macia que se faz ausente

aparece quando o prazer é único, os olhos se encontram

o calor umedece... as partes quentes, que pegam fogo

 chama latente que pulsa, fica dormente a língua que suga

sua rosa negra que é lúdica na minha brincadeira adulta

vem!!!

não passa vontade, minha Preta... deixa tudo e vem!

TRENCHES

in your sumptuous curves
corporeal trenches
eternal desire
which overflows and drops
whispers
shivers that
your skin presents
under my mischievous touch
that your pleasure nurtures.

TRINCHEIRAS

em suas curvas solenes

trincheiras corpóreas

desejo perene

que em gotas transborda

sussurros

arrepios

sua pele apresenta

no meu toque vadio

que seu gozo alimenta.

i WISH

i wish for

only one love.

which i can enjoy everyday

in which i exhaust myself

without thinking about the exhaustion

just feeling the desire

sliding my hands on your body

smooth

mischievous

only mine

and nobody else's.

QUERO

quero

somente um amor.

onde todos os dias me deleito,

onde todas as noites me acabo

sem pensar no cansaço.

apenas sentindo um desejo

deslizar minhas mãos em seu corpo,

macio,

vadio,

só meu

e de mais ninguém.

CORPOREAL CLOCK

in tune,

in thought

in your black skin that i unravel

in this body i drown with my kisses

i *TRANS*form seconds of desire

into hours.

RELÓGIO CORPÓREO

na sintonia,

no pensamento

na sua pele preta que desvendo

nesse corpo que afogo com meus beijos

*TRANS*formo em horas

segundos de desejo.

DREAMS AND DESIRES

hallucinating is the dream of the last hour
the one that's stronger in the memory
real sensations sprout on the skin
it's flowing, exploding energy

it's cold and my body shivers at six a.m
you talk to me but my mind is blown
our mouths approach, you moan
I'm sudden, whilst soft as the wind.

i feel your desire, our bodies seek each other
a warmth rises to my dry throat, cautious
it lights my fire, I'm laid bare

it's glaring realism, fearlessly i surrender
you hold me, licking me the way i get inspired
you kill the longing for a dream full of desire.

SONHOS E DESEJOS

alucinante é o sonho da última hora
aquele que na lembrança é mais forte
as sensações reais brotam na pele
é energia que escorre, que explode

seis da manhã, aquele frio onde meu corpo treme
você conversa comigo e eu não me atento
nossas bocas se aproximam, você geme
eu abrupto ao mesmo tempo suave como o vento.

sinto seu desejo, nossos corpos se procuram
um calor me sobe à garganta seca, reluto
acende minha chama, totalmente desnudo

é realismo gritante, entrego-me sem medo
você me abraça de manhã, me lambe daquele jeito
mata a saudade de um sonho cheio de desejo.

RIVERS

you are a river that
in naughty fluency
runs through my body,
rip tides with no brake
flowing into my river mouth
better known as "soul".

RIOS

você é um rio que
na fluência safada
percorre o meu corpo,
corredeira sem freio
e deságua em minha foz
mais conhecida como "alma".

EVEN SO

even though your hands are blind
your caresses are bare
and your simple mouth severs
their desire is continuous.

groping through my garments
stealing my dreams
savoring my flesh
and always wanting more.

MESMO ASSIM

mesmo sabendo que suas mãos são cegas
suas carícias são meras
e sua boca simples decepa
é contínuo o desejo delas.

tateando minhas vestes
surrupiando meus sonhos.
saboreando minha carne.
e desejando sempre mais.

WHAT I FEEL

i feel my body tremulous and warm at the same time
a mixture of sensations intoxicating it all
exhaling the scent of my desire as (in) a gale
making me feel yours, all yours, in only one thrill.

i just need to get close to you to feel like stealing your kisses
wild thoughts... i take off your clothes.
i run through deserted streets, howl like a wolf
i just need to look into your eyes, and i can't control the desire.

i turn into a fierce animal, so wild
night mists, bewildered and homeless
wishing a second with you, overnight.

transcending my desire with yours, a voyage.
join thoughts, cumming at the same time.
feeling and drinking the nectar from your chalice.

O QUE SINTO

sinto meu corpo trêmulo e quente ao mesmo tempo
é um misto de sensações que me embriaga o todo
deixando exalar o cheiro do meu desejo pelo vento
fazendo sentir-me seu, todo seu e num só gozo.

é chegar perto de ti e querer roubar-lhe beijos.
pensar safadezas... e ir louco tirar suas roupas.
correr pelas ruas desertas, uivar feito um lobo
é só olhar em seus olhos e não controlar o desejo.

disparo feito um animal sem freio, selvagem
madrugada de brumas, desnorteado e sem casa
desejando um segundo contigo, apenas uma viagem.

transcender meu desejo com o seu, visitar lugares.
unir pensamentos, gozar ao mesmo tempo.
sentir e beber o néctar que encontro em seu cálice.

FILL UP MY MOUTH

i smear myself all over sucking a sweet taste,
full of freshness dripping between my lips
it slips on my hands this crazy love
and i grasp it, not letting it slip away.

fill up my mouth with your warm juice
making me mad, insane... reckless.
i eat your whole body until only the seed is left
sliding on my hands, all nasty.

you seduce me with your crazy style
you hold me hostage with your sweet ways
and you show me you're the one, so i want you all the time.

and i fuck you good, no fear... no restraint
devouring you whole without asking for a bargain
Oh, my sweet fruit... my mango-flavored lil' thing.

ENCHE MINHA BOCA

lambuzo-me todo sugando um doce sabor,
cheio de frescor que escorre entre meus lábios
escorrega em minhas mãos esse louco amor
que pego firme, não deixando que escape.

enche minha boca com seu caldo quente
deixando-me louco, insano... inconsequente.
te como inteira até sobrar só a semente
deslizando em minhas mãos, toda indecente.

você me seduz com seu estilo louco
me deixa refém do seu jeito gostoso
e mostra que és foda, te querendo o tempo todo.

e te como gostoso, sem medo... sem manha
devorando-a toda sem pedir barganha
ahhh, minha doce fruta... meu sabor de manga.

TRANSITION

i feel the desire for change,
the desire of only my skin and hair
intense, extensive, strong,
sensitive
all at the same time.
muscles that dance and play
a sex that grows and screams
when rubbing your tongue against mine
i keep up my lust for life,
in my *TRANS*...formation
welcome!

TRANSIÇÃO

sinto o desejo da mudança,
o desejo apenas da pele e dos pelos
intensos, extensos, fortes
sensíveis
tudo ao mesmo tempo.
músculos que dançam e brincam
sexo que cresce e grita
ao roçar sua língua na minha
sigo no tesão da vida,
da minha *TRANS...* formação
bem-vinda!

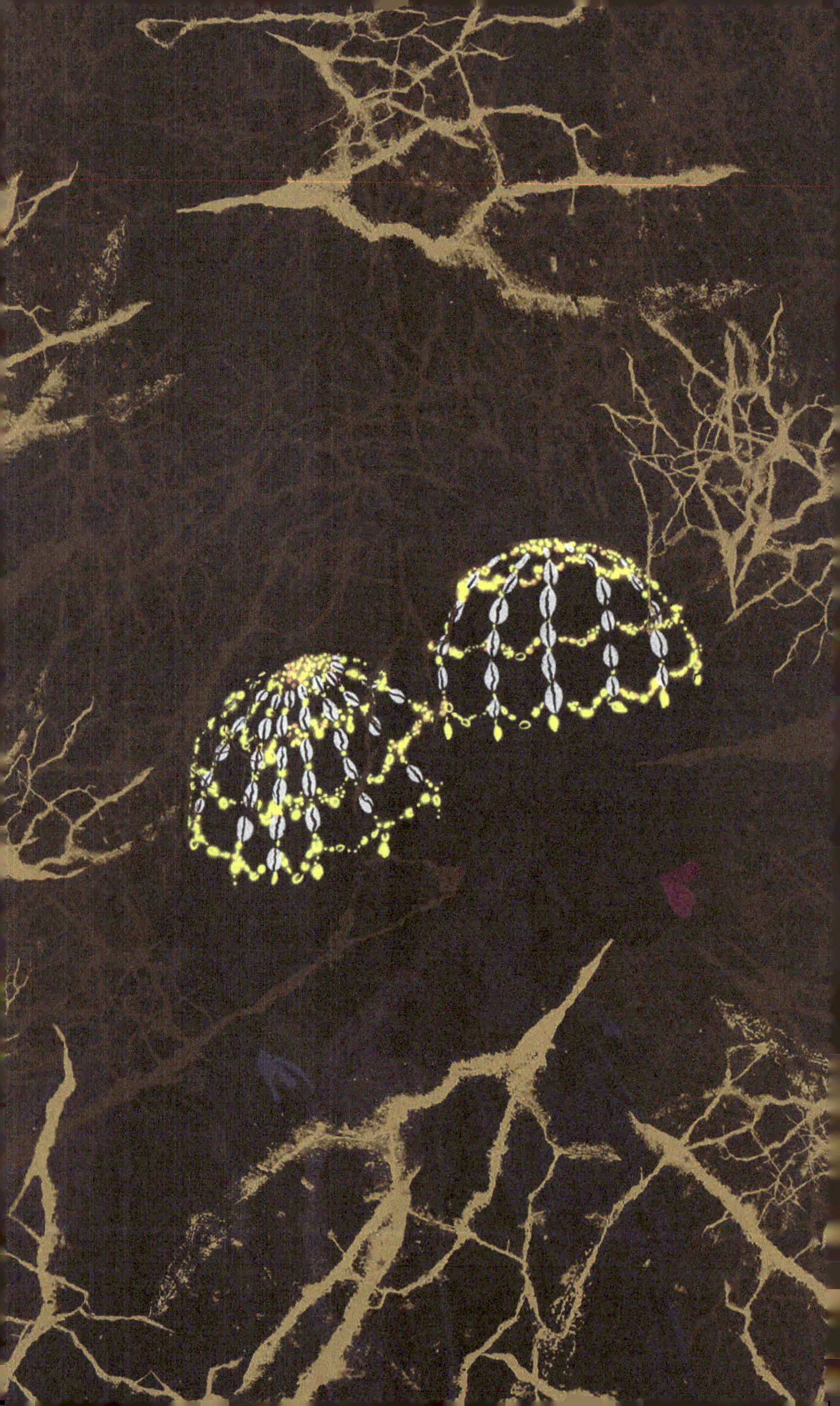

YOUR LAP

in your soft, tasty and fragrant lap
i lose the notion of time licking all over you
sucking energy, strengthening my body
forgetting about life... filling up my mouth.

i fall asleep to the tiredness of loving you so much
only to dream of you.
and in that chimera again i love
your hot body, your black chubby body.

it was you who asked for me, now don't run away
from my thirsty, lustful, pure tongue.
sit on my mouth and feel the heat.

i devour you whole, your entire body
no mercy!
i got you good
with the blind force of a knot
i love you, *Pretinha*
forever and that's all!

SEU COLO

em seu colo suave, gostoso e cheiroso
perco-me no tempo lambendo-a toda
sugando energia, fortalecendo meu corpo
esquecendo da vida... enchendo a boca.

durmo no cansaço de amar-te tanto
que no meu sonho eu sonho contigo.
e nessa quimera novamente eu amo
seu corpo gostoso, pretinho... gordinho.

foi você que pediu, agora não fujas
da minha língua sedenta, lasciva e pura.
senta na minha boca e sinta a quentura.

te devoro toda, todinha assim
sem dó!
te pego de jeito
com a força cega de um nó
te amo, Pretinha
para sempre e é só!

DESIRE

every second this intensity increases,

my desire.

my hands rub frenetically,

a moment of despair,

secret, sacred, let me trace it,

your vibe

your damp body

my wet vulva feeling your heat

on pseudo-pure thin fabric

i wanna transpose your monochrome clothes with my fingers

tear apart all the fabric protecting you from intense cold,

I'm rude

to warm you with my maddened body

I'm so eager

to keep you warm with my mouth forgotten

in your quick release

DESEJO

intensidade que aumenta a cada segundo,
meu desejo.
minhas mãos deslizam frenéticas,
momento é desespero
segredo, sagrado, traço marcado,
seu jeito
corpo suado
minha vulva molhada ao sentir seu calor
no tecido fino pseudo-imaculado

quero transpor com meus dedos suas vestes monocromáticas
rasgar todo o tecido que a protege do frio intenso,
sou bruto
esquentar você com meu corpo enlouquecido,
sou todo ávido
deixá-la aquecida com minha boca esquecida
em seu gozo rápido

TRANSPOETHICALBODY

TRANSforming my absence
POinting towards you
ETHICALly postulating our presence
BODY safe in dreams so true

TRANSpiring what was left of the sparks
POunding explosive desire
ETHICAL, theatrical, tender libido
BODY speaking, words of power.

TRANScribing in Braille, everlasting sensations
POETHICALly receiving your insurgent ship
BODY shivering under your icy touch

TRANScending in your dirty plea…
POETHICALly yearning for your lewd body,
BODY and bravery carrying my desire.

TRANSCORPOÉTICO

TRANSformando minha ausência
CORrendo para seu encontro
POstulando a nossa presença
ÉTICO em meio a sonhos

TRANSpiro o que sobrou das fagulhas
CORrompo-me em desejo explosivo
POtência nas falas, poder na palavra
ÉTICO, cênico, libido amigo.

TRANScrevo em braile, sensações perenes
CORpo arrepia ao toque gelado
POÉTICO ao receber sua nau insurgente

TRANScendo nesse teu clamor safado...
CORagem na volúpia que levo na face,
POÉTICO cobiçando seu corpo indecente.

FLIGHT

under the profane light
she comes with her strong shadow
seeking the ember she swiftly calls
on the other side of the door it crawls
the lock's like a desire that howls
droplets sliding on her body
dripping down her whims,
caresses
loins.
my key is a tongue that never cowers.
throw open this door in fugitive hours.
coming in, invading your body wet
from dirty bathing, dirty thoughts.
a Silhouette that drives me mad
damping my body with sweat.
invading my head
invading my head.

FUGA

no bate e rebate da luz profana
ela vem marcando com sua sombra
buscando a brasa que ligeira chama
que do outro lado da porta emana
a fechadura é desejo que clama
gotas deslizam no corpo desanda
escorre pelas manhas,
carícias
entranhas.
minha chave é língua que não se acanha.
escancara essa porta que na fuga falha.
entra, invade seu corpo molhado
do banho safado em pensamentos.
Silhueta que me enlouquece
transpira meu corpo.
e invade minha mente
e invade minha mente.

FEEL

my kiss
quenches my desire
elevate your soul
listen to my throbbing fire.
and surrender, calmly
your body to mine.
embrace me,
caress me,
feel my Self.

SINTA

meu beijo

mata meu desejo

eleve sua alma

ouça o meu latejo.

entrega-me, com calma

seu corpo para o meu.

abraça-me,

afaga-me,

sinta o meu Eu.

IN MY BED

i want your mouth on mine
satisfying my stray soul's hunger
lay on me,
swim in my river
drown in my body
come back to the surface for air.
breathe, dive, choke,
cry to my soul
and come die in my mad bed.

NA MINHA CAMA

quero sua boca grudada à minha
matando a fome do espírito vadio
que percorre suave a sua língua
deita em mim,
nada no meu rio
afoga-se em meu corpo.
volta à tona e busca fôlego.
respira, mergulha, sufoca,
grita a minh'alma.
e vem morrer na minha cama louca.

HIDEAWAY

it's a secret place
hidden
hideaway
lost in touch
blindfolded.
wet taste
bittersweet lips
both big and small
lost in the shaft of soft words
that stroke
deranges my wet vulva
involved in your delight.

ESCONDERIJO

é um lugar secreto,
escondido
esconderijo
perdido no tato
olhos vendados.
sabores molhados
agridoce nos lábios
grandes e pequenos
perdides no falo da fala macia
que acaricia
alucina minha vulva lúbrica
envolvida na sua delícia.

GOOD NIGHT

that *TRANS*cends in my soul, nocturnal creature

through streets, corners, alleys and villages

endless embraces

avid kisses

that can only stop when the touch is

naughtier

i leave so i don't sleep

in the cold that rules the city

i leave so i don't lose myself

to the desire that wins me

with every look

i exchange with you.

with every touch.

with every word.

BOA NOITE

que *TRANS*borda na minha alma criatura noctívaga

pelas ruas, esquinas, vielas e vilas

abraços intermináveis

beijos sôfregos

que só param quando o toque é

mais safado

vou embora pra não adormecer

no frio que domina a cidade

vou embora pra não perder

pro desejo que me vence

a cada olhar

que troco com você.

a cada carinho

a cada palavra.

LIBIDO

a maddening thought

unstoppable night,

traveling through curves, groin, stretch marks, desire.

a complex drawing in the simplicity of the body

TRANS

vestigênere*

undressed

unmasked

nu… nuances

nudes

selfies… the exchange is mutual

parts of bodies, clicks

pictures and pleasures

we turn to moving pictures

hallucinating in the night with this and that

beginning our adventure exchanging letters

winding up in the agenda we call "libido".

LIBIDO

enlouquecedor o pensamento

madrugada sem freio,

percorrendo pelas curvas, virilha, estrias, desejo.

desenho complexo na simplicidade do corpo

TRANS

vestigênere

desvestides

desnudo

nua... nuances

nudes

selfies... a troca é mútua

partes de corpos, corpas, clics

fotos e gozos

passamos para imagem em movimento

alucinamos na noite com isso, aquilo

iniciamos a aventura com troca de letras

findamos na agenda nomeada "libido".

ANSWERS?

why must we ask questions?
if answers are more alluring
words come out more tempting
in dirty answers blooming?
why must we ask questions?
if your mouth is full and filthy
hot delight that warms my life
so stripped of delight
in these empty nights?
why must we ask questions?
if your answers are more amusing
I'm all giggles, smiling, laughing
lust on my skin, rubbing, and nothing more?!!

RESPOSTAS?

pra que perguntas?

se as respostas são mais seduzentes

as palavras vêm mais indecentes

nas respostas sacanas sementes?

pra que perguntas?

se da sua boca só vem putaria

delícia gostosa que aquece minha vida

sem graça de tudo

nas noites vazias?!

pra que perguntas?

se suas respostas são mais engraçadas

sou só risos, sorrisos até gargalhadas

tesão no pelo, esfregação e mais nada?!!

QUESTIONS

why must we have answers?

if in our questions your gaze wets

my sex that grows, numbs, ravishes

asking for you with shivering pleads?!

why must we have answers?!

if your questions with fleeting glances

out of the corner of your eyes… bring connections… hot drinks…

advances

why must we have stupid answers?!!

if in our questions there's only sex, explosions and colors

naughty lovers, hidden or wide open

why must we have more answers?!

if we're just describing

and it is in our questions that our bodies give back orgasms

PERGUNTAS

pra que respostas?

se nas perguntas seu olhar já umedece

meu sexo cresce, adormece, embevece

perguntando com arrepios em preces?!

pra que respostas?!

se suas perguntas com olhares fugazes

canto de olho... enlaces... bebidas quentes... vorazes

pra que respostas sem nexo?!!

se nas perguntas apenas sexo, explosões e cores

dos amores safados, escondidos ou escancarados

pra que mais respostas?!

se são só relatos

e é nas nossas perguntas que nossos corpos devolvem orgasmos

CORPOREAL

sheets spread
legs entwined
crushed mouths
tongues in wild knots
from that sailor man
or sailor *sapata*
that sucks you to the gut
drowning in a sea of spiders
frantic webs, a ship adrift
our lives lost
are not a river of endless rip tides
we are corporeally lost
in an ocean of love/lovers
that drives us crazy.

CORPÓREA

lençóis espalhados

pernas entre laços

bocas esmagadas

línguas em nó bravo

daquele de marinheiro

ou marinheira sapata

que suga até as entranhas

se afogando num mar de aranhas

desvairadas teias, nau à deriva

nossas vidas perdidas

não é um rio das corredeiras infindas

estamos corporeamente perdides

num oceano de amores

que só nos alucina.

FIRE

it's like a forest fire coming

each step, a shiver

each syllable spoken into my ear

tightens, swells, tightens my vulva

a dance of pleasure,

drenching soft skin… slip in

sliding maddeningly on your indecent skin

a fire without proportions

an entanglement of commotions

ardor, essence, fine mixtures

the scent of vanilla incense heralds

a love that never passes,

always coming back

and warming my empty bed

INCÊNDIO

sensação de queimada chegando

a cada passo, um arrepio

a cada sílaba proferida no pé da orelha

minha vulva aperta, dilata, aperta

é uma dança de prazer,

um encharcar de pele macia... escorregadia

deslizando loucamente na sua pele indecente

é um incêndio sem proporções

um emaranhado de confusões

ardências, essências, misturas finas

um cheiro de incenso de baunilha anuncia

um amor que nunca passa,

que volta sempre

e aquece minha cama vazia

CUE

i'm that actor who forgot his lines.

climbing the ladder of opportunity

in the burning act of mutuality

just waiting for the applause his hands symbolize.

you're my precise cue

just an inconspicuous stare

mouth to mouth so aware

our play in life's theater.

your body is my spike

your mouth leads my step

your tongue is my cue to the abyss

a moat that leaves me adrift

a spark that lights my infinite backdrop curtains.

DEIXA

sou aquele ator que esqueceu o texto.

que sobe a escada da oportunidade

no ato fervoroso da reciprocidade

só esperando os aplausos que suas mãos estampam.

você é minha deixa precisa

apenas um olhar discreto

ou boca com boca desperto

nossa peça de teatro da vida.

sua corpa é minha marca no palco

sua boca é referência do passo.

sua língua é minha deixa pro abismo

um fosso que me deixa à deriva

fagulha que acende minha rotunda infinita.

FLOW INTO

will you flow into me?

torrential gaze

a lust that narrows my eyes

bites my lips

waters my tongue thirsty to suck you

will you flow into me?

your naked neck asking for kisses

a beating bosom whispering smooches

my hands reach for your nipples

i pinch and pinch

will you flow into me?

my beard grazes down your back

all hairs stand on end

i feel you squeeze me

my fingers soak

and you?

you flow beautifully into me...

DESÁGUA

deságua em mim?

caudalosa só no olhar

tesão que aperta a vista

morde a boca

enche d'água a língua louca pra te sugar

deságua em mim?

pescoço nu pedindo beijo

colo lateja sussurrando um cheiro

minhas mãos tateiam os bicos do seu seio

aperto sem parar

deságua em mim?

minha barba desce esfregando suas costas

arrepiam-se os pelos,

sinto o pompoarismo no jeito,

meus dedos encharcam

e você?

deságua linda seu gozo em mim...

MYSTICAL

it's like magic
but it's just lost intuition
it went along with the memory i had
of your breasts rubbing my back
i close my eyes and feel the
sharp tips marking my skin
a shiver between my legs
water flowing down the drain
mixed up with desire, sweat, and cum i open wide
right there
a mystical moment in a lonely shower.

MÍSTICO

parece magia

mas é só intuição perdida,

foi junto com a lembrança que eu tinha

dos seus seios roçando minhas costas

fecho os olhos sinto as pontas

afiadas marcando a pele

arrepio entre as pernas

água que escorre e se perde no ralo

misturada com desejo, suor, gozo escancaro

exato

místico momento do banho solitário.

ABOUT THE AUTHORS

Tiely was born in April 1975. He is a multidisciplinary artist from East São Paulo. He is a member of the Hip Hop generation of the 90s. Tiely has worked/ is working on numerous music and audiovisual projects in which he works to bring visibility to the gender and sexuality debates within Hip Hop culture and the larger Brazilian society. Tiely is a poet, educator, actor, writer, and filmmaker who has worked as an art-educator for more than 20 years. Besides art and education, he is an avid lover of and competitor in sports. Within sports, he is primarily focused on soccer, rugby, and boxing. Tiely has published blogs, articles, essays and poetry. He has also published in academic collections. He is known as Brazil's first nationally recognized hip hop artist who is a Transman.

Jess Oliveira is a translator, poet and researcher. Currently, a Ph.D. candidate in Literature and Culture at Federal University of Bahia, visiting professor in the Department of Spanish and Portuguese (Colorado College), and a research fellow for the Center for Interdisciplinary Women's and Gender Studies - ZIFG (TU-Berlin). Receiver of the DAAD/CAPES (2021-2022) research grant at University Bayreuth, Germany, they hold of a Master's degree in Translation Studies from the Federal University of Santa Catarina and a B.A. in German and Portuguese from the University of São Paulo. Jess works and research focus on poetry and performance across the Black Diasporas. In 2020, they were a finalist for the Jabuti Award in the category Translation. Throughout 2019 and 2020, they were part of the artist residency Rethinking the Aesthetics of the Colony in Johannesburg – South Africa, and of the homonymous platform for translation studies and political imagination across the diasporas. They are a member of Traduzindo no Atlântico Negro – [Translating in the Black Atlantic] at UFBA and part of the cocoruto translationart duo, a platform of experimentation in translation, with Bruna Barrros.

Bruna Barros is a multidisciplinary artist and translator. Associate Researcher of the Research Group Traduzindo no Atlântico Negro [Translating in the Black Atlantic] (UFBA), they hold a degree in English from Federal University of Bahia (UFBA). As a filmmaker, they wrote and directed the short film "Amor de Ori" (2017) and co-wrote and co-directed the short documentary "à beira do planeta mainha soprou a gente" (2020), nominated for the Short Documentary category of Grande Prêmio do Cinema Brasileiro 2021. With Jess Oliveira, they form the cocoruto translation-art duo, a platform of experimentation in translation.

I am Ani Ganzala, visual artist, mother, black, queer, located in Salvador - Brazil, my work revolves around the affectivity and spirituality of black women and queer people.
Photo by Esthefanía Preciado O.